Loon Baby

Houghton Mifflin Books for Children
Houghton Mifflin Harcourt
Boston New York 2011

Loon Baby

by Molly Beth Griffin

illustrated by Anne Hunter

For Emer —M.B.G.

For my husband, Andrew —A.H.

Text copyright © 2011 by Molly Beth Griffin
Illustrations copyright © 2011 by Anne Hunter

Houghton Mifflin Books for Children is an imprint of Houghton Mifflin Harcourt Publishing Company.

www.hmhbooks.com

The text of this book is set in Caxton.
The illustrations are done in watercolor and ink.

Library of Congress Cataloging-in-Publication Data
Griffin, Molly Beth.
Loon Baby / by Molly Beth Griffin ; illustrated by Anne Hunter.
p. cm.
Summary: A baby loon, afraid that his mother will not return, sets out on his own to find his way across a
stormy lake to their home in the great north woods.
ISBN 978-0-547-25487-6
1. Loons—Juvenile fiction. [1. Loons—Fiction. 2. Animals—Infancy—Fiction. 3. Mother and child—Fiction.]
I. Hunter, Anne, ill. II. Title.
PZ10.3.G88074Loo 2011 [E]—dc22 2010006770

Manufactured in China
LEO 10 9 8 7 6 5 4 3 2 1
4500267106

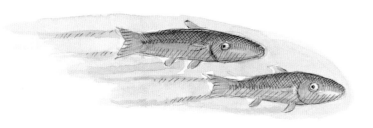

In the great north woods
by a little round lake
in a soft, warm nest,
a baby loon lived with his mother.

One day at suppertime
they left the nest
and swam out to the middle of the lake.
Mama Loon dove for Baby's dinner—

ker-splish!

—and she was gone
under the rippling waves.

Loon Baby waited
and floated
and paddled in circles.
The breeze ruffled his fluff.

He stuck his head under the cool waves to look.
Nothing but green lake-light.
His mother was far off finding their supper,
and Loon Baby couldn't follow.
He couldn't dive—
not yet.

So he waited
and floated
and paddled in circles.
The breeze ruffled his fluff,

and the little loon wondered . . .
Had Mama met a moose?

Had she fought with a snapping turtle
and flown far away?

She had never been gone
this long before.

Loon Baby had to find his mother,
so he ducked his head under the water
and kick-flipped with his feet.
Suddenly there he was
in the green lake-light . . .

but not for long.
Loon Baby just bobbed back up,
and still no Mama.

He dipped under to try again—

Each time he bobbed right back up,
and by now he was sure:
his mother was not coming back.

and again—

and again—

So Loon Baby paddled in a slow, sad circle,
all alone on that big, chilly lake.
The wind picked up and tore at his fluff,
and a cold rain began to fall.
He forgot all about dinner
and started to paddle toward home.

But which way was home?

Poor Loon Baby—
tired and hungry,
cold and wet and lonely,
and *lost*.

After so much diving,
so much bobbing,
all of the shores looked the same to him—
just pines and rocks and marsh grass.
His nest could be anywhere.

Loon Baby wailed a cry,
a high-low shuddering cry,
a mournful, wavering cry,

a sinking, giving-up cry.
The cry shook his whole body
and shivered out over the whole empty lake.

But then—
a black head!
A red eye!
A white checkered back!
Up slid his mother!

Loon Baby peeped

and flapped

and splashed,

then gulped his dinner down.

Then, before they headed home,
despite the wind and despite the rain,
despite the cold and despite the coming dark,
Loon Baby dipped down and—

ker-splish!
—he dove
    deep
        under the rippling waves.

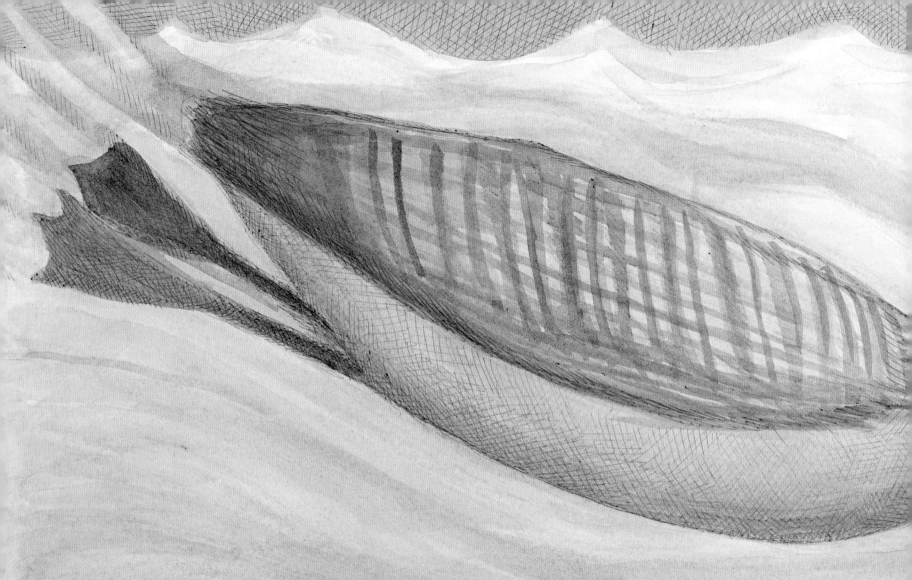

Mama ducked down too,
and together
they kick-flipped
through the green lake-light,
all the way home . . .

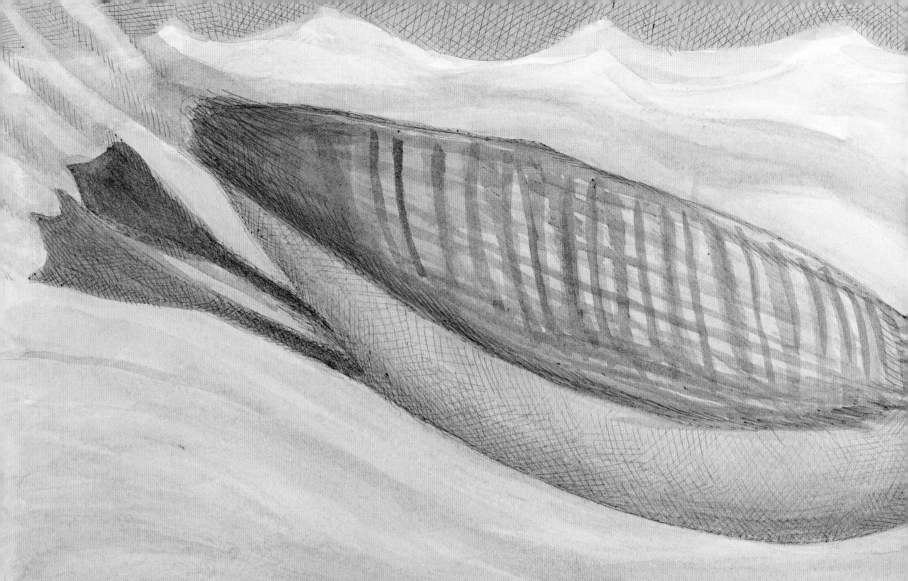

Mama ducked down too,
and together
they kick-flipped
through the green lake-light,
all the way home . . .

ker-splish!
—he dove
deep
under the rippling waves.

to their soft, warm nest
by the little round lake
in the great north woods.